SUSAN WILLIS is an author living in Birtley, Co-Durham. She has ten novels, seven novellas, and a collection of short reads.

Writing Psychological Suspense and Cosy-Crime novels with strong, lovable North East characters, is her passion.

Susan also writes stories for Woman's Weekly magazine.

All her work is available on amazon here:
https://amzn.to/2S5UBc8

The characters, premises, and events in this book are fictitious. Names, characters, and plots are a product of the author's imagination. Any similarity to real persons, living or dead, is coincidental and not intended by the author.

Also By Susan Willis:
A Year of Short Stories
Payback at the Guest House
Confession is Good or the Soul
Intriguing Journeys at Christmas
Joseph is Missing
Death at the Caravan Park
The Curious Casefiles
Magazine Stories from the North East
Christmas Shambles in York
Clive's Christmas Crusades
The Christmas Tasters
The Guest for Christmas Lunch
The Man Who Loved Women
Dark Room Secrets
His Wife's Secret
The Bartlett Family Secrets
Northern Bake Off
You've Got Cake
A Business Affair
Is He Having an Affair
NO, CHEF, I Won't!

Chapter One

"All three bodies were lying on their backs perfectly straight with their feet pointing towards the door. Formally laid out. As a doctor might lie out his patients."

I read this and shiver. Gosh, Agatha Christie sure knew how to put the jeepers-creepers up her readers. I'm reading, The Monogram Murders, while sitting on the back seat of the coach which is taking us to Washington Old Hall to take part in a murder mystery weekend.

It's been a longish journey from home and although I've been absorbed in Agatha's story, I'm now beginning to feel a little restless and need to stretch my legs. I've eaten my sandwiches and I stare out at the drizzle running down the coach window. I am with other members of our writing group and I peep around the side of the seat in front of me.

Jane and Stephen are sitting together, and I smile. As husband and wife, they often remind me of two peas in a pod. They're both in their late forties and seem to have morphed into one. They always sit together in the group and I often watch them with their heads bowed sneaking secretive smiles at each other. They agree about everything and praise each other's writing to such an extent that I feel the stories could be jointly written. The plots, storylines and characters are often identical to each other's.

'Hey, you two,' I say.

Stephen turns his head to face me. 'Not long now, Linda,' he says grinning. 'We'll soon be there.'

I smile and feel a tremor of excitement flutter in my stomach. 'Oh, I hope everyone enjoys this weekend, Stephen, especially as it was my idea.'

Jane leans across Stephen and claps her bird-like hands together. They often flutter when she talks animatedly in class. 'Of course, we will, don't worry, we'll have a great time!'

In July, when I'd returned from The Harrogate Crime-Writing Festival, I'd been full of ideas and told the group about the amazing authors who had spoken about their work. Harlan Coben and James Pattinson had been there from America entertaining us with their background tips for writing about crime. I'd plotted three cosy crime stories using up to date social topics about poor mental health and the perils of social media.

'There's always a reason why people behave the way they do,' I'd said enthusiastically to everyone. Therefore, it had been unanimously decided to concentrate the next four group sessions on writing crime and mystery.

We've been reading and discussing, Agatha Christie, PD. James, Ruth Rendall and other authors loosely described as the golden age detectives. Our homework had been to write a short mystery story and, for mine I'd chosen to use the powers of deduction.

I love Sherlock Holmes. Whether it be the old Sherlock "Basil Rathbone" or the new Sherlock "Benedict Cumberbatch" I'm hooked on all the stories. I like to examine things and try to think of a conclusion based on the facts, although I never seem to come up with the same deductions which Sherlock does.

Everyone had enjoyed my story when I read it out in the group but compared to some of the other writers I had felt as though I hadn't quite grasped the mysterious side to the genre. It seemed to me as though I was trailing behind everyone. The following day I spotted the advertisement for a murder mystery weekend and thought it would be great to get involved in our very own murder scenario. Many group members had commitments therefore couldn't spare the time, other than Bob, our leader, Jane and Stephen, and Jenny who only joined the group two months ago.

I crane my head further around the seat to see Bob sitting further down the coach in quiet discussion with Jenny. Bob is a young seventy-five year old man and an inspirational writer. He is bright and clever and can whizz through a crossword in minutes. He's been running the group for eight years and was very welcoming when I first joined at the beginning of the year. I close my eyes and remember that day in January.

I'd been writing for seven years and had a few successful stories and novellas published, but often found that writing was a solitary experience. Therefore, I found my nearest writing group and registered my interest. Standing outside the room in the local library that morning I had taken a deep breath. Were these writers more advanced and accomplished than I was? Maybe they were more creative writers, whereas my writing had ranged from romance to writing cosy women's magazine stories. I'd chewed the inside of my cheek and pondered whether to go in or turn around and hurry home. Pulling my shoulders back, I strode inside probably looking more confident than I had felt. They'd been twelve writers around the table. After I'd been introduced to everyone, I breathed a sigh of relief.

I hadn't been out of my depth and loved the conversation and discussions of everything bookish from that very first day.

However, now I know everyone well. Probably, the only person I don't know a great deal about is Jenny. She seems very nice and is always pleasant to us all in a conversational manner, but she doesn't talk in depth to anyone. Other than Bob.

When she'd given her small introduction to us all, she had said, 'I'm looking at ancestry websites because I was born in an Irish convent and adopted. I would like to trace my birth mother and her family.'

We'd all wanted to know more but she'd shuffled her papers together and stopped talking. I figured it would be rude to probe for more information when she obviously hadn't wanted to elaborate.

I can see Bob stand up and pull his overnight bag down from the rack above and I wonder how we'll all get along together for the next couple of days? We enjoy each other's company in the two-hour sessions we spend together, but how will the dynamics of the group work over three days?

The coach pulls onto a long driveway and I look out of the side window hoping to catch my first glimpse of the 17th century manor house.

Chapter Two

Linda

I follow Stephen and Jane down the steps from the coach and gasp looking up at the house and Jacobean gardens. It's huge - so much bigger than I thought it would be for some reason. I had imagined a high squat building with turrets and higgledy-piggledy floors of bedrooms, but the manor house is only three-storeys high. It is spread out with what looks like arms of rooms in different directions. Maybe these are the guest wings, I think and decide to write down these descriptions when I get to my room.

At the end of the arm towards the east is a smaller building and I wonder if this is a little chapel to the side of a wide set of sweeping stone steps. It is all built in a pale brown brickwork with terracotta roofs. I grin knowing Bob will probably correct me later with the proper masonry and building terms. Men like Bob always seem to know these things especially as he once told me how he'd been a structural engineer before retirement. Not that I know exactly what this entails but I figure he'll know all about buildings.

I hear Jane behind me squeal with delight and turn to see her fluttery hands tugging at the silk scarf around her neck. She's obviously excited, I muse and grin at her. 'It's amazing, isn't it?'

She giggles. 'Oh, Linda, we're going to have such fun!'

It's dusk and the bright Autumn sunlight has disappeared which gives the place a misty-murky atmosphere. I shudder. This impression would be perfect for a spooky ghost story set in a forest. Already my mind is buzzing with verbs and words to use in my writing.

I come up with these descriptions, *the trees waft in the breeze. The fog settles around them like a blanket. The noise of a fox scratting in undergrowth. Shadows in the fog creep up the side of the house. A macabre sinister feeling hangs around us all.*

I grin. To experience a place like this will make it easier to write from first-hand knowledge and I determine to jot down as much as possible over the weekend.

I'm startled from my thoughts by Stephen calling, 'Hey, Linda, look at these!' The drive and courtyard are covered in heaps of leaves. Stephen bends forwards onto the grass and gathers a handful. 'I so love autumn colours,' he says. 'Look at the different shades of orange and red.'

I hear the coach driver calling to us and we hurry towards Bob to collect our luggage. A member of staff in a traditional costume walks through the gateway towards us. Bob greets her and we follow them both into the reception based in the square courtyard.

***

My bedroom is beautiful. I've walked into the room and dropped my case to the floor completely stunned at the Jacobean décor. I perch on the edge of the four-poster bed and grin. Apparently when I reserved the rooms there'd been a mix up and they'd over-booked one room. Therefore, the others are on the first floor, but the hotel have upgraded me to a deluxe room on the second floor. I had offered the room to the others, but they'd insisted that I take it, so I have, and I'm thrilled - it's fabulous. All the soft furnishings are a reddish tartan check and there is a long curtain to pull around the wood carved posts of the bed. Hmm, I think, pity I'm on my own in this huge bed and giggle.

I walk to the window and there is just enough light to see that my view is across the front of the manor house overlooking the gardens, a clump of tall trees and a small pathway. That looks like a nice walk in the morning, I think and spin around to look at the old stone fireplace. Opening my case, I grab my toilet bag and hurry through into the bathroom. I gasp. A roll top bath and large walk-in shower greets me and I sigh in pleasure.

After a quick shower, I change into a black skirt and red turtle-neck sweater, make a coffee and sit down at the small writing desk in front of the window. I open the welcome pack and read the itinerary for the weekend.

Your Group Murder Mystery Weekend with Ms Cynthia Roberts

1, Some character roles in our mysteries are played by a few in-house members of staff.

2, Your role during the events is to act as an investigator and clues will be spread out throughout the house

3, Question the suspects. Watch the incidents. You may discover a body or two!

4, You won't be required to act but may be put into teams of investigators

5, The action may unfold around you. Take the opportunity to interrogate the suspects

6, You can freely walk around the manor house and talk to characters in the restaurant and study rooms

7, The events will be continuous throughout the weekend so be careful you don't miss anything!

8, Bring a note pad and pen with you to jot down things you may hear or see. Listen carefully to what the suspects say they may have something to hide. Read the evidence against them

9, Be suspicious and watch the characters' facial expressions which may give away guilty secrets. Stay alert. Keep your eyes and ears open

10, Most of all enjoy yourself and have fun

Your scenario this weekend will be:

1, A successful businessman is having an extravagant event to celebrate his new product release and you are invited. Who is the beautiful blonde woman sitting in the corner? Is she his new girlfriend? Who is envious of him? Would somebody kill through jealousy?

I hoot and grin to myself. This is right up my street and I imagine running around all weekend investigating like

Sherlock. I turn back to the front page and notice my name, Linda Stevens is at the top of the agenda which presumably is because I made the booking.

I'd noticed a scowl from Bob in reception and he'd even tutted when I'd been given the deluxe room. I wonder if he thought as leader of the group he should have had the room. I frown and think of the last few group sessions.

Lately, and for some reason, although he's very pleasant to my face, I get the feeling he resents some of the comments and suggestions I make in the group discussions.

I remember the saying, some men struggle to take advice and opinions from a woman. Hmm, I wonder if this is true of Bob and if he'd been like this with his wife and two daughters?

I glance at the clock on the fireplace and realise I'm five minutes late for dinner downstairs. Cursing under my breath, I grab my bag and hurry out of the room.

Chapter Three

Bob Thompson

Jenny is a nice lady and all, but she is very full on. She talks at length about emotional scarring, whatever that is supposed to mean. I think it's one of these modern-day sayings which everyone associates with having upset in your life. I scoff. These days everything must be analysed and talked about openly. Whereas, in my day, we just had to get on with it and cope the best way we could.

I pull the zip along on my overnight case and frown. For some reason Jenny had attached herself to me when we got on the coach. I've also noticed at the writing group how she always makes a beeline to sit next to me, even though I'm not the only bloke. We have Jimmy, Stephen and Peter, but she never sits next to them. Only me.

I sigh unpacking my things and hope she isn't reading more than there is into our friendship. I hang up the two shirts I've brought. Maybe I have shown too much interest in her family search and, what I think of as encouragement, she has taken as something completely different. Women do have these fanciful romantic notions, but I'm too old to start all that up again - aren't I? Although I don't know for certain what age she is, I figure she must be at least ten years younger than me, if not more.

I head into the bathroom and put my shaving kit in the small cabinet. I rub my chin deciding I don't need to shave until tomorrow morning. Apart from anything else, I couldn't even think about starting a relationship with another woman. It's only twelve years since I lost my wife, Joan.

Now, I sigh wistfully, she was the best woman ever. She knew me inside out. As I did her. I couldn't have loved any other woman more than I did Joan. I swallow down the lump of emotion which always gathers in my throat when I think of my wife.

I shake myself from the melancholy mood and head into the bedroom to read the agenda for the weekend.

A few months ago, in the group session Linda had suggested, 'Why don't we try a few months of writing different genres like Sci Fi, historical romance or crime fiction?'

I'd felt the teeniest bit annoyed. I run this group, I thought, and, although we've welcomed any new members to join, I object to newcomers who wanted to dictate their opinions to everyone. 'Well, it's something we could look at,' I'd said. 'But I think you'll find we all write in whatever genre we choose because that's what we are used to doing.'

Stephen had said, 'I think it's a great idea, Linda, it'll shake us all up a bit and I like nothing more than a challenge. So, shall we do a Brexit and put it to the democratic vote?'

There'd only been two of us who weren't fully committed to the idea. But overall, the majority had agreed. Most members had wanted to try something different. What's wrong with the way I've always ran it, I'd wanted to cry - you've never complained before. We've always written in any genre we like because I'm dedicated to prose and poetry.

However, later that day, I decided it would be an experiment and attempted to write a mystery. When I had finished the story, I'd been delighted after reading it aloud to my oldest daughter. She'd said, 'That's great, Dad. We should all be able to recognise the value of change in our lives.'

More of this contemporary speak, I'd thought, but at the same time tingled with pleasure at her praise.

I think of my two daughters. The oldest, who looks so much like Joan it makes my heart squeeze every time I see her, and my youngest, whose kind gentle personality is just like her mother's. I wonder what they'd think if they knew about John? I shudder at the very thought and try to push my son out of my mind.

I've been able to do this for the last two years since I found him. But lately, he keeps creeping into the back of my mind which niggles at me. Maybe, it's with Jenny joining the group and delving into ancestry sites and tracing family histories, because that's how I found out about him. I'd been in the library and a friend had told me it was free to look at a popular ancestry website. Eagerly, I had delved into my family backstory. After a few sessions over the coming days, I retrieved print outs of my grandparents' and, great grandparents' lives. I'd also found old friends and colleagues from my time spent in army barracks near London.

One close friend had a sister called, Susan who I remembered immediately. I traced them both and then stared in horror at the name of a baby boy on a birth certificate. I'd felt physically sick knowing the birth date and the name John couldn't be anyone else's but mine. The skin on my neck prickled and I'd felt my cheeks flush when tracing him on social media. The photograph of him on Facebook as a happily married man with two children made me gulp hard and gasp. There'd been no mistake. It had been like looking into a mirror and I'd known he was my son.

I remembered Susan and the great three days I spent with her in London on leave. I also remembered the lies I told her when we'd first met. 'My name is John Donaldson,' I'd said and looked into her big trusting eyes. 'I'm from a big house in Northumberland where my family have a very profitable business.'

She'd looked suitably impressed. Whereas, the actual truth was I had been christened Robert and was raised in the slums of Newcastle from where I'd been glad to get away and enlist in the army. It had been three meals a day and I got warm decent clothes to wear.

Of course, I had meant to find Susan when I left the army. But when I found work in Gateshead, met Joan, and fallen head-over-heels in love with her, Susan had been wiped from my mind.

I sit on the edge of the bed and frown. Thankfully, Joan had never known anything about my son John. It would have been a double blow for her if she had found out because we'd tried to have a son but both attempts had resulted in miscarriages. And, knowing my wife she would have made me get in touch to find out for certain if he was mine. Joan valued family above everything else in our lives.

Deciding there isn't time to make tea, I bounce slightly on the mattress and know it is comfortable and soft enough to support my back. I glance at Linda's name on top of the agenda and wonder what her bed is like upstairs in the deluxe room. I'm not sure how she managed to get upgraded when I'm in charge of the group.

Maybe it was because her name was on the credit card which had reserved the rooms at reception. But, I grunt, some people always come up smelling of roses.

Chapter Four

Linda

I hurry along the landing and glide down the enormous wooden staircase covered with a beautiful carpet runner and brass stair rods. I smile holding the carved handrail and appreciate the grandeur which reminds me of the film "Gone with The Wind". Not that I have the ballgown Vivien Leigh wore, but I grin, a girl can always dream. I stop near the bottom in front of an enormous gold leaf mirror and look at myself. A little over five foot two with a blonde bob and what I think of as slanted green eyes, I know I'm nowhere near as beautiful as the actress, but I pull my shoulders back determined to enjoy every minute.

I hurry inside the dining room and gasp in awe. Two huge glittering chandeliers hang from the centre of the room and I smile at the beautifully decorated round tables. A member of staff ticks me from his list and shows me across the room to join the others. I smooth my palms down the sides of my skirt and wish I'd worn something a little more stylish. Taking a sigh of relief, I see Jane wearing smart but casual wear too.

'Isn't it fab?' I gush, and sit down next to Stephen.

Stephen nods and hands me the menu. 'Oh yes. And it looks like we are in for a scrummy dinner too.'

Discussions take place over everyone's rooms. Stephen and Jane have requested a twin room, and Jenny and Bob are in single rooms towards the end of the corridor. Everyone agrees the rooms are clean and very comfortable.

Bob turns to me. 'So, I suppose your room upstairs is much bigger?'

I see his big bushy eyebrows draw together and can hear the resentment in his voice. I choose to ignore this and finger the dessert spoon. I look at him directly. 'Well, although I haven't seen the size of your rooms, I figure it will be,' I say.

'But I did offer the room to everyone when we were in reception.'

He grunts as a waiter appears and begins to pour wine into our glasses. The waiters are all dressed in jeans with white shirts and tartan waistcoats.

Jane breathes wistfully. 'I love the tartan everywhere, don't you?'

'I suppose it's okay,' Bob says, sipping his wine. 'Although we are all a bonny long way from Scotland.'

Jenny joins in the conversation. 'It's not meant to be Scottish,' she says. 'It's what is called, Country Living.'

I smile at Jenny. 'Yeah, I've stayed in some hotels when I've been working and they do this too.'

'The worlds gone mad,' Bob utters.

I see Stephen and Jane raise their eyebrows simultaneously because they are well used to his grumpy ad hoc comments, and I giggle.

I hope the wine might cheer him up a little and I turn towards Jenny. She is a very large lady in her early sixties, I'd guess. Her face looks quite pale surrounded by short grey hair and big round black glasses. I've often thought the glasses looked too big and heavy for her small face. She pushes the bridge of her glasses up her nose and smiles back at me.

'I hope we get time to talk more over this weekend, Jenny,' I say. 'It's always so busy and full-on in the group sessions that we've never had a chance to get to know one another properly.'

'Yes, I'd like that too,' she says.

The meal is delicious and the wine goes down a treat, although I notice Jenny only drinks water.

At the front of the dining room is a small platform. After a tinkle of a spoon on glass silence descends upon everyone. Ms Cynthia Roberts, the organiser of the murder mystery weekend, steps up to speak. She's a tiny woman with a pixie blonde hair-cut and purple glasses. She explains the plans for the weekend. These include rules and regulations of the manor house and she sounds like a school headmistress. We all listen attentively just like her pupils would do. She points to a clipboard with a map and four columns in red marker pen. Apparently, there are two groups of twelve friends. One group of eleven friends. And our group of five. Our first task is to give our group a name.

While everyone mutters around the room. I decide it might improve Bob's mood if I let him take the lead.

I whisper, 'Bob, what do you think? I mean, as our writing group leader, I think you should give us a name.'

Bob pulls back his shoulders and I can tell he's chuffed.

'Hmm,' he says, leaning forwards onto the table making a steeple with his fingers. 'Well in our library at home we are affectionately known as, The Jotters, so how about that?'

Jenny claps her hands together. 'Oh, that's fantastic, Bob - I love it!'

I grin at them all. 'Me, too. Then everyone will know we are writers.'

Cynthia asks the leaders of the four groups up to the platform to write our names on her clipboard, and Bob heads off towards the platform.

I watch him put the name on the clipboard and then Cynthia takes him aside. With his balding head lowered to Cynthia's level, I can see she is talking quickly and explaining something on the columns. Bob turns to shake hands with a tall thin man who looks in his mid-fifties. They both turn towards us and arrive at our table.

'This is Owen,' Bob says. 'Cynthia has asked if we wouldn't mind him joining our group to even the numbers out a little. Apparently, the activities work out better with even numbers.'

We all nod enthusiastically towards Owen.

Jenny says, 'Nooo, of course we don't mind. Come and have a seat with us.'

I smile at him and he walks around the table to sit down next to me. Maybe he can see how Jane and Stephen are together, as is Jenny and Bob, and I'm the odd one out. Which I suppose in one sense, is true. He places his bottle of lager on the table and sits down while I turn towards him and introduce myself.

'Well, I'm single now and a member of the writing group,' I say. 'It was my idea to come on the murder mystery weekend because we've been studying the golden age detectives.'

I suddenly wonder why I thought it was necessary to tell him I was single, and smile. He looks nice with gold rimmed glasses and short brown hair. If I had to think of a word to describe his looks it would be studious.

'Me, too. I mean, I'm single as well. This weekend was arranged by my friends and it was supposed to be a bit of a blind date. Another woman was due to come to make up the six partners, but she cancelled last night,' he says. 'I'm not sure what that statement says about me.'

I giggle. 'Oh, that's not kind,' I say. 'I wouldn't do that to anybody, but, look at it this way, you could have had a lucky escape?'

My cheeks flush realising I'm being too familiar and how he might not appreciate it. 'Sorry, I shouldn't have said that. I mean, you might have been really looking forward to meeting her and be disappointed. Plus, of course, she could have a perfectly valid reason for cancelling.'

He nods and grins at me. It's now that I notice his piercing blue eyes behind the glasses. They are small eyes but warm and friendly, and they seem to be laughing with me.

'What?' He asks. 'Like she's been mysteriously murdered and is still lying in a pool of blood waiting to be discovered by Hercule Poirot!'

I throw my head back and howl with laughter and he laughs too.

Owen tells me how he runs a book club and that the new detectives in TV dramas are his favourites. 'But I'd give anything to meet my much-loved Rebus in a Glasgow pub for a shot of whiskey.'

I smile and tell him about my love of Sherlock and, how I like to examine the clues and guess at who-dun-it scenarios. He says, 'Ah, but it was the butler, wasn't it?' We both laugh and he reels off his other favourite crime writers.

I move the spare cutlery away from the edge of the table to rest my elbow. 'They all seem to be old detectives with flaws in their characters?'

He takes a mouthful of larger and nods. 'I think the best ones always are. Afterall they are only human beings like us all.'

I nod. 'Ian Rankin, who wrote Rebus was at the crime writing festival in Harrogate when I went - it was a brilliant weekend.'

I tell him all about the weekend and he pulls a small notebook and pen from his corduroy jacket pocket to jot down the details.

In his soft Welsh accent, he says, 'Well, it would be a bit of a trek for me because I'm from, The Valleys.'

His voice is like treacle flowing over me and I feel my knees quiver. My lips feel damp and realise I have my chin resting in my hand staring at him. I'm so completely hooked by his words I'm in danger of drooling.

I hear Stephen shout across the table, 'Linda! Don't you be hogging our new team player we all want to hear about him.'

Startled, I nearly fall off my elbow and mumble an apology, sit back in my chair and drain the wine from my glass.

Owen begins to join in the group conversation about the manor house while Bob reaches over and pours more wine into my glass.

I thank Bob and see his eyes are twinkling. He's obviously cheered up with the wine.

I watch and listen to Owen discussing the building with Jane. He sounds quiet and reserved in their company. But now I know he is amusing when he's on his own, I decide this weekend is going to be even more fun than I'd thought it would be.

I join in with everyone. 'I wasn't sure of the correct name for the pale terracotta brickwork, Bob?'

Everyone turns to look at Bob who shrugs his shoulders. 'Why would you think I'd know that?'

I frown. 'Because you were a structural engineer,' I say. 'So, I figured you'd have some idea about the building.'

Bob shakes his head briskly. 'Em, I'm not sure where you got that notion from, Linda,' he says with his lips pressed together in a grimace. 'I've never been a structural engineer.'

I look at the others for confirmation, but Stephen and Jane have their heads down and as a new-comer Jenny wouldn't know his background.

Owen intervenes. 'Maybe you've got Bob mixed up with someone else at the group?'

I can't help furrowing my eyebrows and I shake my head.

Bob gives a small snigger towards Owen. 'Women, eh,' he says. 'Don't you just love them?'

I bite the inside of my cheek knowing if I snap back it will be embarrassing. I turn my head away from him and gulp at my wine. I cross my arms and clench my jaw, not just at the fact that he's blatantly told a lie, but more at the derogatory comment about women.

Jenny makes an excuse of tiredness and leaves to go to her room. I shuffle on my seat further around towards Owen and away from Bob. I know it's best to keep my distance if I don't want to lose my temper.

Jane begins to look around at the old paintings hanging on the walls. She is the history buff in the group and loves to read historical fiction. She talks about each one as we all follow her vision and give our comments about the scenes and colours. I mention the three big paintings which are hanging on the staircase and we decide they could be the ancestors of the house. 'Apparently, they incorporate parts of the original medieval home of George Washington's direct ancestors. There are displays on George Washington, and how the Hall was saved with American support,' she says.

I notice Bob seems to have shrunk back into his chair and remains quiet as the two waiters appear offering us coffee and biscuits.

We all order but Bob stands up.

'Well, it's been a longish journey, so I'll make myself a coffee in my room and finish my book,' he says.

We all say goodnight as he shuffles out of the room and then continue to talk about the agenda for the murder mystery.

Chapter Five

Linda

Although I'd felt tired after the long journey, I had lain awake for a while waiting for something to go bump in the night. I'd pulled the tartan curtain around the four-poster bed wanting to feel part of the old Jacobean atmosphere, but it had felt spooky and scary being closed-in by the heavy material. So, after ten minutes, I had drawn it back again. The wind had strengthened since we'd arrived, and it howled against the old windows making eerie noises. I'd lain with the quilt pulled up under my chin staring into the pitch-black darkness.

It had felt much different to my flat at home with a streetlight outside the bedroom window. Eventually, I'd decided, although it was supposed to be atmospheric, I would rather have a glimmer of light in the room. Old pipes had clanked from the room next door which only added to the creepy ambience, but this was nothing to what had happened next. Just as I began to drift off to sleep, the couple in the next room began to have noisy intimate relations. I figured it had to be noisy for me to hear them through the thick walls. As she'd cried aloud and howled louder than the wind at the windows, I'd pulled the quilt over my head and gritted my teeth. Oh, goodness,' I'd muttered. 'He can't be that good!

Now, it's morning. I'm showered and dressed in my jeans with a green jumper. My ex-husband told me when we first met that I should always wear green because the colour complimented my eyes. It was one of the nicer things he said to me over the years before he ran off to Cyprus with his business partner. Cliché, I know, but it did happen.

I shake myself back to the here and now. I think of seeing Owen and hum a little tune whilst skipping around the end of the bed. I'd thought I was going to be the odd one out in the group this weekend, but now I have a partner in crime, I think and giggle. And, he just happens to be a nice-looking guy around my own age who is fun to be with. I smile and head downstairs for breakfast.

***

When I see Owen sitting at our table chatting to Jenny, I call out, 'Morning.'

As I approach the table, Owen pulls out the chair next to him. Hmm, nice manners too, I think while admiring his blue fisherman's sweater.

'We are waiting for the others to come before helping ourselves to the buffet,' Jenny says eyeing the hot dishes under big silver tureens.

'Oh, I wouldn't think anyone would mind if we ate now, Jenny,' I say.

Jenny hot-foots it to the long tables covered with white cloths and an array of cereals and breads.

Owen nods and sips his coffee. A waiter appears and pours hot coffee into my cup.

I inhale the roasted bean aroma. 'Aaah, I could do with his,' I say.

I tell him about the shenanigans last night in the room next door and make it sound amusing.

We discover, his room is five doors down the corridor from mine. 'Well,' he says. 'It wasn't me. I don't think I could make any woman howl for more!'

I laugh out loud while he jiggles his eyebrows in a comical manner and then laughs himself.

When Jenny arrives back to the table with a heaped plate of bacon, eggs, sausage and beans we head off to the buffet table.

I have my normal muesli and toast. I smile noticing Owen has chosen the same. And, that's another thing we have in common, I note tucking into my breakfast.

Stephen and Jane hurry into the room apologising for being late and a discussion takes place about it being unnecessary for breakfast timings because the agenda doesn't begin until ten. I can see Owen looking from Jane to Stephen as he tries to understand how they seem to speak as one and finish each other's sentences.

Jenny lowers her head next to my ear and says quietly, 'What was that all about last night with Bob and his job?' I'm not sure how to answer. Do I tell her Bob has lied about his career before retirement? And if I do, will she tell Bob what I've said because they do seem very close. I frown not wanting any ill-feeling over the weekend, so I reply, 'Oh, it was nothing, Jenny, simply a misunderstanding.'

She nods and attacks the sausage with her knife. She cuts a large slice and chomps on it slapping her big lips. 'This is one of the best sausages I've ever had! In fact, I may just have to have another,' she says, and heads off to the buffet table.

Bob has arrived and greets everyone sitting down next to Jane. While everyone discusses their night's sleep, I stare at Bob and wonder why he did lie about his job.

'Penny for them?' Owen whispers in my other ear.

Bob has gone off to make toast at the buffet table. I shrug my shoulders and tell him about Bob. We are talking quietly so I know no one will overhear us. 'I just wonder why he's telling lies,' I say. 'I mean, why lie about your career?'

Owen smiles. 'Well, in my experience lies are usually behind guilty feelings about something.'

I nod. 'Yeah, but why would he feel guilty about being a structural engineer?'

'Well, Sherlock, maybe he had an unskilled job in the company and had always aspired to be an engineer,' he says.

I smile at his joke and decide to ask some of the older group members at the next writing session who may know the answer.

Stephen breaks through everyone's conversations by waving his printed agenda in his hand. 'Oh, I'm longing to get stuck into this,' he says. 'Has anyone had thoughts about the successful businessman?'

'We've made a few notes already,' Jane says opening her handbag and lifting out a small notebook and pen.

Bob clears his throat noisily as if to bring the group to attention. He says, 'I wondered if we are going to stay in three pairs to do the exercise? Or, shall we investigate as a group of six?'

Jenny wipes her mouth with a napkin. 'Well, I think it would be better to search for clues in pairs,' she says looking at Bob and delicately tilting her head to the side. 'And if Bob is okay pairing up with me, that would be great.'

I see Stephen and Jane nod their heads at the same time. I look at Owen and holding my breath, I ask, 'So, are we okay to pair up together?'

Owen looks around at everyone and then rests his gaze on me. 'I couldn't think of a nicer sleuth to work with.'

I grin at him, thankful he hasn't refused because it would have been embarrassing.

Stephen claps his hands together. 'Splendid!'

'Well,' I say gleefully. 'That means, if I'm the detective I should work towards eliminating the murderer by grouping the suspects together and then discounting them one by one.'

Owen grins. 'And I'll be happy to play the side-kick, Doctor Watson to your Sherlock,' he says jiggling his eyebrows together again. 'Of course, I'll notoriously go off in the wrong direction!'

Everyone laughs at his him. I feel a lightness in my chest and my mouth dries ever so slightly as we all make our way into reception. I stand to the side of the group and stare at Owen's back in his denim jacket. His shoulders and chest are broad which makes me feel secure and comforted in some way. I swallow hard recognising the feelings of desire from many years ago when I first met my husband. But now, was I falling for Owen? The hairs rise on the back of my neck and I shiver, but it's not with cold.

Chapter Six

Linda

I'd been expecting Cynthia to be in reception to tell us what to do but she isn't here. Instead, a tall beautiful blonde woman glides across the black and white tiled floor and perches on a high stool in the corner. Her long blonde hair is flowing over her shoulders and she parts her pink sweetheart lips to smile at us all. She is dressed in a pale blue silk suit which highlights her baby-blue eyes. The skirt is cut just above her knee and she crosses her long slim legs seductively. I hear two men standing to the side of me audibly gasp in appreciation.

Owen whispers in my ear. 'And here is our Marilyn Monroe look-a-like.'

I wonder what colour her lipstick is and then nod at Owen. 'Yeah, well, I can see how lots of men would be jealous of her boyfriend,' I say, and smile. 'I suppose we must find out if someone would kill through jealousy and, if so, who?'

'It says the clues are spread throughout the house so shall we head off and investigate, Sherlock?'

I giggle. 'Come on then, Doctor Watson, let's look for some characters to question.'

We spend the whole morning looking around the study rooms and chatting to members of staff who offer more clues as we try to put the pieces together. The further through the house we progress the easier and more relaxed I become with Owen. We laugh and talk together as if we're old friends. I realise we have the same sense of humour and are very similar in many ways.

We stop in one of the larger rooms and grab a coffee. With the help of Owen's outstretched arm, I perch on a high stool to drink my coffee while he stands next to me sipping his.

I have my notebook in my hand. 'This sent a shiver up my back when I read the card,' I say, and try to whisper in a more spooky tone, '*You are not alone. Don't forget to lock your door at night!*'

Owen laughs. 'We'll probably have wacky dreams about all of this when we get home.'

I nod. 'I know, but I'm writing all the evidence and clues down to add into my stories when I get home.'

He smiles. 'That's a good idea.'

I gulp at my coffee. 'I seem to be constantly asking questions and querying everything that happens. So, I'm wondering if this is because I'm studying crime,' I say. 'I mean, I don't think I was as inquisitive when I was writing romance and historical stories. Although I do remember one of the crime writers in Harrogate saying how asking questions moves the plot along in a story.'

Owen rubs his chin. 'It probably does,' he says. 'That's how we find out the answers by investigating from the clues we've been given. And, by the way, I'm loving talking about crime and murder all the time. Does that make me a weirdo?'

I laugh. 'Well, if it does then so am I - because I'm loving it too!'

There is warmth in Owens smile when he says, 'I so admire anyone that can write. I'm an avid reader but wouldn't know where to start writing a book,' he says. 'In fact, Linda, I'd love to read some of your work?'

Now my cheeks feel very hot and not just with the warm coffee. I appreciate his interest in my writing, but is he just being kind? Or does he genuinely want to read my work? I open my purse and give him one of my business cards with social media links to my books. 'Well,' I say. 'You can find them on Amazon if you do want to read some.'

'Brilliant,' he says, and tucks my card into the back pocket of his jeans.

We head off again on the character and clue trail. I love how the rooms are furnished in Jacobean style with a fine collection of oil paintings, delftware and heavily carved oak furniture and wood panelling. The old flowery carpets give off a slight musty smell and when I push open the big carved wood doors to the library, I gasp in delight. 'Oh God, I could live in here, Owen. This is my idea of heaven!'

He nods enthusiastically and strides ahead to look at the row upon row of old books. 'I bet there's a few old Sherlock Holmes copies in here somewhere,' he teases, and swings around to face me.

I can see happiness shining in his eyes and I grin. 'Me, too, it's amazing!'

Owen steps towards me and his cheeks blush. 'I just want to say, Linda, that I wasn't particularly looking forward to this weekend when my date cancelled, but now I'm so pleased she did,' he says shuffling his feet together. 'Because I couldn't be happier with my new partner in crime.'

I gulp and feel my throat dry at his words. Is he feeling the same as me? I sigh, is it so long since I've had a compliment that I don't know how to react anymore, and can't think of what to say? I stutter slightly, 'W…well, yes, I'm really glad she cancelled too.'

We stroll around the library wide-eyed at the display of books. 'Is it too cliché to find a body in the library?' Owen muses, 'I'm sure Agatha Christie has a novel called just that.'

I step up close behind him and peer over his shoulder at a whole shelf of books dedicated to the golden age detectives. 'Yeah, I think she may well have.'

I can smell the hint of a sandalwood aftershave around his neck and I hear him take a deep breath. It is lovely to feel so close to him.

Suddenly, I hear a loud, 'Co-eeee.'

I spin around to see Jenny entering the library. 'We are all hungry now,' she says. 'So, we're going to have lunch. Are you coming?'

I hurry towards her feeling Owen close behind me.

***

We have joined the others around the table in the dining room to have a buffet salad lunch.

Stephen strokes the side of his moustache and asks, 'So, how is everyone getting along with the clues?'

I look at Owen not sure how much, if anything, we should give away. Afterall, it is a team game and I've always had a competitive streak. I raise an eyebrow at him.

'Ah,' Owen says fingering the side of his glasses. 'Now that would be telling because we are as thick as thieves!'

Jane almost shrieks at his pun and her hands flutter enough for her to drop her knife. Everyone laughs.

I watch him spread butter onto a baguette. Owen is so quick-witted, I think tucking into my salad. And, the more I'm around Owen the more I like him.

Bob lays his knife and fork together onto his plate. 'Well, without sounding like I'm bragging I think I've got this one all sewn up!'

I stare at him wondering how he could possibly do that. He wouldn't have had time to race ahead in every room for the clues. And, I notice how he hasn't included Jenny although he is supposed to be sleuthing with her.

'Really?' I say.

I stop myself from questioning him more because I don't want to make another blunder, but I needn't have worried.

Stephen bursts out, 'But how?' He asks, 'Have you been on a pair of roller-skates, Bob?'

Jane giggles and I smile at Stephen hoping he will challenge him further.

Bob puffs out his chest and then clears his throat noisily. 'No, I've just gathered the evidence quickly and gone from room to room at speed. I didn't need to hang around debating,' he says. 'The mystery is all very straight forward actually.'

'So, did the butler do it?' I ask. 'Or, was the body in the library?'

We all laugh together. Well, everyone except Bob who frowns at me.

I turn to Jenny. 'And do you agree with Bob as to who the murderer is?'

Jenny pushes a large piece of ham into her mouth and chews noisily. 'Well, he hasn't told me, and we sort of lost each other after the third room,' she says. 'But I'm sure Bob will have nailed it.'

I hear Stephen click his tongue in annoyance and he raises an eyebrow at me. I know he is thinking the same that poor Jenny has been wandering around the manor house on her own. I chew the inside of my cheek. If Owen hadn't joined our little group I might have paired up with Jenny, and this doesn't seem fair.

As if Owen has read my mind, he says, 'Well, if Bob is finished sleuthing for the day and has found the body, Jenny, then you must come with me and Linda this afternoon.'

I smile at him and look up to see Cynthia approaching our table. She asks, 'So, how are we all getting along?'

Jenny pulls her shoulders back. Her eyes are bright as she points to Bob. 'Well, our leader Bob has solved the mystery already,' she says.

Cynthia raises a fine pencilled eyebrow, 'Well, I'm not sure how he can do that because the dead body character hasn't been placed yet.'

Bob's thick bottom lip wobbles. 'No! I haven't,' he says. His cheeks flush bright red. 'I didn't say that I'd found the body!'

We all stare at him. Cynthia smiles, turns on her high stiletto heels and hurries over to the larger group.

I get up to leave. I don't want to be involved in the following conversation with Bob. I turn to Owen, 'Are you coming, Doctor Watson?'

Owen grins and steps up behind me then places a hand gently on Jenny's shoulder. He opens his mouth to speak but Bob interrupts gruffly. 'No, Jenny can stay with me.'

Chapter Seven

Linda

We are one of the first pairs to find the body in a small study room next to the library. Owen was heading back towards the door when I noticed two feet clad in brown brogues sticking out from behind the sofa. I cried, 'Owen, look!'

'Apparently,' I say reading the card. '*The body is of the businessman's ex-partner who has remained a good friend to him.*'

'Hmm,' Owen says bending over the body. 'Or has he?'

I look over my shoulder but we are the only people in the room, so I know we can talk freely without being overheard. There is more evidence on a card tied around the ex-partner's knee which Owen reads in a whisper, '*I know what you did, and I hope you get what you deserve!*'

I laugh and look at the character's expression. 'I think he's died a painful death because his face is all scrunched up with his eyes closed.'

Owen nods. 'Well, we can't interrogate this suspect like we have done the others because he's dead,' he says. 'But the card does tell us how the door is locked from the inside, so there must be another way out of this room.'

Owen begins to walk around the walls running his hands over the wallpaper. I watch and copy what he is doing although I'm not entirely sure of what I'm looking for. Owen is near the fireplace and shouts, 'Linda, over here!'

He has found a lever behind a small portrait next to the mantle. He pushes and pulls the lever which finally creaks open to reveal a small doorway. I feel a shiver run up my back as I follow behind him into a long narrow passageway. It is dark and has an old mouldy smell. We are in complete silence and my eyes adjust to the darkness. Tentatively, I take a few steps. My mouth dries and my legs tremble a little, but

I spot a dim light up ahead so know it doesn't look too far to walk.

Owen holds his hand out behind him. 'Take my hand, Linda and be careful where you put your feet,' he says.

I grasp his hand feeling so glad he is with me and say, 'I…I'm not great in confined spaces.'

Owen reassures me. 'It's only a short passageway, just keep tight hold of me and you'll be fine,' he says, and squeezes my hand. His hand feels strong and capable, and I sigh with relief slowly following in his footsteps.

When was the last time a man had supported me like this, I wonder? I've been on my own for so many years now I've taught myself how to be self-sufficient in everything I do. But all the same, I grin, it's lovely to have a man to lean on again.

We reach the light and walk up a few steps outside into daylight and a hazy-grey sky. There is an eerie stillness with only the sound of birds tweeting. I blink my eyes and Owen turns around to face me.

He takes his glasses off and wipes them on the bottom of his sweater. When he puts the glasses back on, he looks directly at me. 'You alright, Sherlock?'

I giggle and nod. 'Thanks, Owen. I don't think I would have done that without you. If I had been with the others, I probably would have bottled out and missed this clue off the agenda altogether.'

He smiles. 'I'm not sure if we should have been in that passageway because no one else has - it looks like it hasn't been used for years,' he says.

'Hmm, maybe not,' I mutter.

He looks animated and I can see in his face how he must have looked as a small boy.

He grins. 'But I couldn't resist the adventure of not knowing where it would lead to!'

I smile and look around. 'I wonder where we are?'

He looks past me up ahead. 'Come on, there's a trail here through the trees.'

I realise I'm still holding his hand, but don't want to let go. My heart is beating fast and I feel charged up ready for anything. I'm loving our unforeseen adventure and know I'll note all of this down later. *It's murky amongst the trees and some of the branches look like tendrils of a monster reaching out, and over us. The only noise I can hear is a few twigs snapping as Owen treads over them. There's a damp earthy smell to the vegetation.*

I shiver. Although I'd been warm enough inside the house, I wish I had brought my jacket.

Owen obviously feels me shiver and drops my hand to remove his jacket. 'Here, take this, I'm warm enough,' he says, and drapes it around my shoulders.

'Nooo, then you'll be cold,' I say.

However, he has already headed off walking along a gravel path which has appeared to the left.

I hurry along to catch up with him pulling the denim jacket further over my shoulders. The collar smells lightly of his aftershave and I smile. Just past the trees the path opens out into a clearing with an old outbuilding. We both stop in our tracks. Owen stares with an open mouth.

I gasp. 'Oh, how lovely,' I say. 'I think this is what's called, a folly.'

Owen turns to me with shining eyes. I can see he's excited and enjoying our escapade. 'Yes, Linda, I think you're right, but now-a-days we'd use the word, summerhouse.'

I grin and pull back my shoulders. 'No, Owen, the difference being is that this building is made of stone and has no purpose. Follies were built as ornaments in parkland or gardens whereas summerhouses are built for people to use.'

He laughs and we hurry towards the old round folly. There are three well-worn steps up to the door which are over-grown on the sides with foliage. Another evidence card is tied to the handle. He whispers, '*I'll remember who you are, and you will see me again!*'

'Ooooh,' I say, and laugh.

We open the old door which creaks and enter the room. There's only muted light and the room seems gloomy but in the corner is an old stone bench.

'Ah, just to prove me wrong there is a seat in here,' I say, and head over to sit on the bench. It's a high seat and I swing my legs back and forwards. Owen joins me.

We sit in silence for a while and my mind goes back to lunchtime and how Bob had behaved. I purposively haven't mentioned it to Owen but now I do.

'You must think we are a strange group,' I say. 'But usually we are quite normal. I could never have imagined Bob would act like this.'

Owen rests his head back against the wall. 'It's okay, we have some strange characters in our reading group too.'

I chew the inside of my cheek. 'It's just that I can't help noting all the inconsistencies in his words and actions now, but maybe this is because I know now that he tells lies.'

'Hmm,' he smiles. 'I think from all the mysteries I've read, people are rarely straightforward and readers do love a good liar in their stories.'

I smile thinking about his words. 'That's true, but I would never have thought Bob could be someone who fabricates the truth,' I say. 'Although, I only know him from our writing sessions once a fortnight whereas the others have known him for years.'

'Well, maybe they aren't surprised at his actions because he's often like this. You could always ask them tonight over dinner?'

I nod and shake the thoughts from my mind.

We get up and walk slowly back along the path but choose the opposite turning. This takes us past the Nuttery and orchard, arriving back onto the front of the house.

'Ah, this is the view from my window,' I say. 'When I first arrived, I saw this path and thought it would make a nice walk.'

I look up at the windows and count along pointing out my bedroom to Owen. 'That's mine there.'

He does the same. 'And mine is the one on the end with the side window.'

I look at him with his head turned up and smile. I feel a lightness in my chest and know it's a comfort to have him near me.

Chapter Eight

Jenny Turnbull

We've had another nice dinner in the restaurant tonight. The food is very good. Almost too good for my enlarging figure. I've always had a problem with my weight but lately it has escalated out of control and I don't know how to stop it. A niggle in the back of my mind says, just stop eating, but as my old Mum would say, 'That's easier said than done.'

I strip off my clothes in the bathroom and avoid looking in the wide mirror above the bath. Hurriedly, I pull my nighty over my head. No need to upset yourself any further, I think and push my feet into my slippers.

I head through to the bedside table and pull the quilt back but don't climb into bed. I perch on the end and cover my face with cream. It's supposed to stop wrinkles, I chortle, but at sixty-seven, I'm never going to have a skin like Jane Fonda. I'd been a school dinner lady all my working life, so have never had the money to spend on expensive face creams, but I smile, it does feel nice when I rub it into my skin.

I puff up the two pillows and climb into bed sinking cosily against them with my book on top of the quilt. I place my mobile on the bedside table and switch on the TV with the remote control. Although I don't intend to watch TV, I like to see the light reflected in the room. I've never liked total darkness at night but know if I leave a lamp on it will disturb my sleep.

I sigh and think of everyone at lunchtime and the rumpus I'd caused by telling Cynthia that Bob had solved the mystery.

I'd felt awful afterwards. It had seemed by boasting about him that I actually embarrassed him which had been the last thing I wanted to do. 'I'm so sorry, Bob,' I'd mumbled. 'I thought you'd said you had found the body?'

'No, I didn't!' He'd almost growled.

But Stephen and Jane had spoken up. 'We thought the same as Jenny because by saying you'd solved the mystery it meant that you had also discovered the body.'

I felt relieved I wasn't the only person who'd misunderstood Bob. There had been an awkward silence until Jane had changed the conversation by talking about one of the characters and the evidence cards.

I also noticed at lunch how Linda and Owen left straight away before further discussion took place. I smile thinking of them both and how Owen offered to take me with them in the afternoon. They obviously didn't want me to be alone which was kind.

They seem to be getting quite close and I'm glad because they'd make a nice couple. I've always thought it was a crying shame how Linda was on her own. She deserves to have a nice chap alongside her, although from all accounts her husband had been a rotter. Owen is clever and funny, and I can see he makes her laugh. He makes me laugh too.

I reach for my glasses then belch loudly and pop an antacid chew into my mouth. I rub the crampy ache which is starting in my left arm. I've had it a few times now but I'm not sure what it is because I haven't injured my arm. Probably arthritis, I think, but decide to see the doctor when I get home. I had thought of making a doctor's appointment last week, but I'd been so excited planning this weekend it had slipped my mind. My thoughts had been full of preparations about the time I would spend with Bob.

I like Bob very much. And up until this weekend, I'd thought he felt the same for me. I reckon I've sort of hero-worshipped him. As the leader of the group he is organised, he oozes confidence in himself, speaks well in a crowd and appears to be very knowledgeable on many subjects, especially writing. Everyone looks up to him and he is the total opposite to my shy introverted personality.

But, I sigh, from leaving home I've seen a different side to him. A side, that to be honest, I'm not that keen on. I'd sat next to him on the coach and within twenty minutes I got the distinct impression he hadn't wanted me to share the seat. He'd shuffled about looking around at everyone. Where in the past, he'd been all charm and very engaging, on the coach he'd been indifferent and paid scant attention to my conversation. I had been confused and a little hurt by his attitude.

Later, I'd hoped to find out more about his background when I asked Linda about the misunderstanding with his previous career. Obviously, she hadn't wanted to tell me anymore about the kerfuffle. And ever since has looked as though she wants to give him a wide berth. And I don't blame her, because now I know he does tell lies, I feel the same myself. He'd also told me he had been a structural engineer.

I frown knowing I should have stuck up for Linda when she tackled him about the transgression, but I've never been keen on confrontations and always shy away from any arguments. I shake my head and tut. I was definitely in the wrong and should have supported her. Maybe, I'll talk to her in the morning and explain properly and, apologise.

Also, I grimace, until this weekend I hadn't realised that Bob was so short tempered. He seems to be on edge most of the time and if something doesn't go his way, he becomes agitated and hostile to those around him, which on this weekend just happens to be me. When we were deciding upon who to pair up with in the group, I'd asked Bob to sleuth with me. Not that I'd wanted to spend any more time with him, because by then I hadn't, but it meant Owen would have to join up with Linda. And now, I'm pleased I did.

I close my eyes and remember joining the writing group. It had been four months ago after my ninety-five year old mother died. I'd hoped it would help to plug a big gap in my life that caring for Mum had left. And to some extent, it had helped. I'd been interested in the ancestry description on the poster in the library and, although I've never written anything before, I was encouraged to join the group.

I've always known I was adopted and how Mum got me from a convent in Ireland. Apparently, or so Mum told me, my birth mother had been from a staunch catholic family, and my birth father had been a protestant. When she became pregnant, she hadn't been allowed to marry outside of her faith and had been cast out by her family. In those days, the popular saying had been, never the twain should meet.

When I'd explained my story to Bob, he'd recommended I watch the film "Philomena" with Judy Dench, which I'd done. We had talked at length about tracing ancestry before the group sessions. We also had a coffee in the library together where I got the impression that like me, he'd not been in hurry to go home to an empty house.

I'd said, 'It's just that I'd like to know more about my birth mother who will most likely be dead now, but I'd love to know if she had any more children. I mean, what if I have half brothers or sisters?'

He'd nodded sympathetically. 'Yes, Jenny, you'd want to know that at least,' he'd said. 'You could have another branch of your family living somewhere in Ireland!'

It was during these talks I had the feeling he'd tracked his family on ancestry mainly because he knew so much about it and their website. Although, I sigh, he never actually admitted as such.

I rub my arm and open the first page of my book. I begin to read and shiver at the author's first sentence. *You're mine now and I love to watch you sleep!*

Chapter Nine

Linda

We are all gathered around the table having finished breakfast. Well, everyone except Jenny who hasn't arrived yet. The dining room is nearly empty at nine o'clock and I figure the other groups, who'd had a lot to drink last night, are hung-over.

I'd had a great time with everyone last night, especially with Owen. We'd had a delicious dinner followed by a few hours of fun and laughter. Owen had told everyone in a funny manner how we'd discovered a secret passageway which hadn't been on the agenda. 'I'd gone off in completely the wrong direction looking for another way out of the library,' he'd said.

I joined in by stating, 'Well, you are my side-kick and they notoriously get confused, Doctor Watson.'

He'd laughed. 'I know! Cynthia hadn't even known the passage was there and if she had it would have been against Health & Safety regulations to include it in the agenda. So, we are never going to win the competition now that I've cocked-up!'

Everyone had laughed and enjoyed themselves. Even Bob had looked happier when he'd entertained us with amusing anecdotes. Whether I'd believed any of his tales, I wasn't sure.

Towards the end of our coffee and biscuits, Owen whispered to me, 'I'm thinking I might go up to the North East again for a weekend trip?'

I'd held my breath.

'I'm a huge fan of Antony Gormley who designed The Angel of the North and I'd love to see the sculpture.'

I had simply nodded in agreement and smiled. Had it been an excuse to see me again on another trip? Or did he simply want to see the sculpture? Part of me felt apprehensive because our relationship was progressing at an alarming rate, but the bigger part of me had felt excited at the thought of seeing him again.

He'd walked me to my room and stopped outside the door. I'd read the signs. We'd leaned in close to each other and he'd stared into my eyes. His eyes had softened as he'd gently stroked his finger down my cheek. I thought he was going to kiss me, and my heart began to race, but he'd simply bid me goodnight. I'd swallowed hard and watched his back as he'd headed along the corridor towards his room.

Stephen breaks my train of thought now. 'I wonder where Jenny is? It's not like her to miss a big fry-up breakfast.'

'She's probably just slept in. I'll send her a text,' Bob says. He plays with a loose blue thread on his jacket where a button had once been. They are the brass naval type of buttons and I can't remember it being missing before? I suppose it could have been and I just hadn't noticed.

I look at Jane as she yawns. 'You look tired - did you not sleep well?'

She tuts and waves a hand towards Stephen.

On cue, Stephen takes up the conversation. 'It was my fault because I had a wobble during the night,' he says. 'I was convinced I felt a hand on my shoulder shaking me awake.'

'Really?' I say looking from one to another.

Stephen nods. 'Well, it seemed so real - I'm not a fanciful person and don't believe in ghosts or anything supernatural, but I'd swear there was a big hand on my shoulder gripping and shaking me,' he says shivering, and rubbing his arms. 'So, I went and sat on the edge of Jane's bed and woke her up because I was rattled by it.'

Jane snorts. 'Yeah, but I calmed him down and reassured him that there was no one else in our bedroom. He got back into his own bed but that wasn't the end of it all,' she says raising an eyebrow at Stephen to continue.

Stephen laughs now. 'So, just as I was dozing off again there was a soft but distinctive cooing noise,' he says. 'It seemed to last for ages, OOOOOOO. I sat bolt upright in bed with my heart banging.'

Jane says, 'And that was when I really did lose my temper and shouted, it's just a bloody owl! Go back to sleep!'

We all burst into laughter. I can feel Owen's shoulders shaking sitting next to me as he belly-laughs and then makes the same cooing noise.

'There's a story in that just waiting to be written, Stephen.' I say.

I look up to see Cynthia hurrying towards our table. I can see concern in her eyes as she stands in front of us smoothing her hands down a black pencil-skirt.

'Morning,' she says, and then begins to gabble. 'It's about your friend, J...Jenny. It's just that we can't get an answer from her room and it's locked from the inside. The cleaners had started at the far end of the corridor this morning and the girls have knocked and knocked but she's not answering?'

Bob scrapes back his chair. 'Oh dear, I've sent her a text, but she hasn't answered.'

I look at Owen who shrugs his shoulders.

Jane's hands start to flutter and she pulls at the red polo neck on her jumper. 'Are you sure she's in there?'

Cynthia nods and grips hold of the back of Owen's chair. He swivels around to look up at her.

'She must be in there because the cleaners can hear the television,' Cynthia says. 'But I do need permission to use the spare key to enter her room.'

I get up and pull on my jacket. 'Well, yes, I would think that would be the right thing to do,' I say, and look at everyone for confirmation. 'We should go and see if she's alright.'

Everyone nods and we follow Cynthia out of the dining room.

***

When we reach room seven a woman wearing a pink tunic is waiting outside with a key in her hand. All our keys are attached to a block of wood with the number marked in black. The cleaner twirls the key in her long fingers looking at Cynthia who nods her consent.

I can feel Owen behind me as a shiver runs up my back. For some reason I have a feeling of imminent trouble settle over me. Something doesn't feel right. Something is wrong. I shake myself and look at Cynthia who raises an eyebrow as she pushes open the door.

I follow Cynthia and the cleaner into the room. The curtains are pulled but the bedside light is switched on making the room appear shadowy. Breakfast news on the TV is reporting from Downing Street. I stop abruptly behind Cynthia nearly treading on her black stiletto heel.

The cleaner screams and puts her hands over her mouth. I look past them both to see Jenny propped up against the pillows. Her face is waxen and slightly bloated. Her head is lain backwards on the pillows and her eyes are wide open staring at the ceiling.

I hear Owen behind me whistle through his teeth. 'Jeez…'

Cynthia moans and approaches the bed. I follow behind her knowing even from this distance that Jenny is dead.

Cynthia mutters, 'Is she breathing?'

'I…I don't think so,' I say, and pat Cynthia's arm.

There is complete silence now. All I can hear is Bob's thick boots tread on the carpet while he approaches the other side of the bed. Then Stephen and Jane appear behind him staring down at Jenny.

'Oh my, God,' Stephen whispers.

Cynthia shoos the cleaner out of the room and snaps, 'Go and find the hotel manager immediately.'

I turn my attention back to Jenny. Her mobile is clutched tightly in her hand and I look down at the blank screen knowing the battery, like her, is dead. There is a psychological thriller novel opened on the quilt cover which she'd been reading and her big glasses are lying next to it. I stare at those trendy glasses which I've always thought were too big for her cute little face. I stifle a sob in my throat as the enormity of what has happened hits home.

I can feel Owen's breath on the back of my neck because he is so close to me.

He murmurs, 'But, no one can die unexpectantly on a murder mystery weekend, can they?'

We all look at each other and shake our heads as if we want to chorus "of course not". Everyone, including myself, looks decidedly uncomfortable, as if in some way we are responsible for her death. But I know this is crazy and I rub the back of my neck. If anything, we may be guilty of neglecting and not paying her enough attention, but that is all. I swallow hard and my chin quivers.

I stare down at her mobile. 'Oh, how sad,' I say. 'Maybe she was trying to contact one of us if she wasn't feeling well?'

There is sudden noisy activity in the corridor and two men enter the room. Cynthia introduces a short chubby man in a black suit who is the hotel manager. Bob nods at him.

'Now, this is a sorry situation,' the manager utters. 'I've sent for the emergency doctor and the police.'

The manager almost propels a young lad forward towards the bed. 'But in the meantime, this is an ambulance driver who is staying in the hotel.'

'I'm Jason,' the young lad says looking around at us all.

I try to smile at him but my face feels frozen and I can't manage. Jason seems to be around twenty with a spotty but eager young face.

He strides up to Jenny on the bed and puts his head on one side near her mouth. He nods. 'Well, she's definitely not breathing.'

And then he places his hand on her forehead and nods again. 'She's cold. I'd say she's been dead for hours.'

Jane whimpers and Stephen puts his arm along her shoulders. I feel Owen put a hand on my shoulder and squeeze it.

Bob mumbles, 'Dear, God.'

I reach forward to lift her glasses from the quilt, but Jason stops me. 'Don't touch her or anything in the room,' he says. 'Leave everything the way you found it for the police in case she has died in suspicious circumstances.'

I gulp at his words, suspicious circumstances and feel my shoulders tighten. Owen rams his hands into his pockets behind me and makes a slight grunting noise.

We all stand in silence not knowing what to do as Jason follows the hotel manager and Cynthia out of the room. The palms of my hands are clammy and I begin to shake uncontrollably. The only sound in the room is a tap dripping in the bathroom sink which sounds as loud as a waterfall.

Chapter Ten

Linda

We all gather in the bar sitting around a low circular table. Jason had mentioned contacting Jenny's next of kin, so Bob has arrived back from his room with his writing group file. He starts to flick through all the paperwork looking for any other contact details. His usual rosy-cheeked complexion has gone and his face is pale. I reckon he is feeling as anxious as we all are. He draws his heavy eyebrows together and frowns. 'Nope, I've got nothing other than Jenny's mobile number. I don't even know her home address!'

I sigh and look around the empty bar area. None of us are remotely interested in the weekend's activities anymore. I hear the other groups creeping around in the study rooms talking about their clues and look at Owen sitting beside me.

'It's a shame you're missing out on the rest of today's sleuthing,' I say. 'If you want to go off and find your friends, I'm sure they'd let you join in.'

Owen shakes his head. 'No, my heart's not in it anymore, Linda. If it's okay, I'll stay right here with you.'

I feel a warm hug of comfort from his words which helps to quell the anxiety in my knotted stomach. There's a strained atmosphere between us all. Jane's hands are fluttering as she delves into her handbag for a tissue. Stephen is tapping the toe of his loafer against his chair which makes me grit my teeth.

In times of stress, I often have a giggly reaction and confess this to Owen. I whisper, 'I'm thinking of the scene in Faulty Towers with Basil and the kipper,' I say. 'The episode where the man is already dead and Basil places the breakfast tray in front of him!'

Owen shuffles on his seat and I see him stifle a snigger.

I gulp, and feel dreadful about poor Jenny dying alone and feel my cheeks burn. 'Gosh, that was a terrible thing to say,' I whisper to him. 'I didn't mean it!'

Owen nods and takes my hand in his. 'I know you didn't,' he says. 'Don't worry, we'll soon know what's happened.'

With his kind words my eyes fill with tears and I swallow hard. My bottom lip trembles. I look around at the others who are still sitting in silence. 'I...I feel so sorry that Jenny died here on her own and, I wish I c...could say sorry to her,' I stutter.

I can't stop the tears falling down my cheeks now. I brush them away with the sleeve of my sweater. 'I'm even sorry I asked her to come on the weekend. I mean, if she'd stayed at home, she'd probably be alive and well this morning!'

'I think you could do with a brandy,' Owen says, and squeezes my hand. He gets up and strides off to the small bar.

Bob shakes his head. 'Linda, that wouldn't have made any difference, because I do know Jenny lived alone,' he says. 'Therefore, she probably would have died on her own at home anyway.'

I know he is trying to make me feel better and I nod miserably.

Owen returns and hands me a small glass. 'I...I don't think I like brandy,' I say, but take the glass from him with trembling hands.

He nods. 'Just sip it slowly and it'll make you feel better,' he says giving me a big smile.

I take a couple of sips and a slow deep breath. I feel the warmth of the alcohol flood through my system and I manage to relax my shoulders.

Cynthia pops her head around the door. She looks tired and drawn. She is wringing her hands together and I stare at her purple nail polish. 'The doctor is with Jenny now and the police have arrived. I know you're all anxious to know what's happening but all I can say for now is that the doctor reckons she died around two o'clock this morning,' she says. 'I'll be back when I know more.'

We all look at each other. I can see everyone is calculating where they were at that time.

Stephen mumbles, 'It was around that time I woke feeling the hand on my shoulder. If only I'd known Jenny was ill, then I could…' he says, but doesn't finish his sentence.

Jane buts in. 'Yeah, and that's when we heard the owl hooting because I looked at my bedside clock.'

I sigh. 'I never moved all night,' I say. 'I was exhausted and with the extra glasses of wine I just zonked out.'

I look at them all. Surely none of them could have had anything to do with Jenny's death. I've known them all for months now and none of them seem capable of doing such a thing, but, are they?

I sly a sideways look at Owen. He was with me in the bar until midnight talking and drinking. He did escort me to my room, but really, what do I know about him? With my Sherlock hat back in place, I wonder: if Jenny has died in suspicious circumstances what motive would Owen have? I chew the inside of my cheek and finish the brandy. Maybe, it could have been someone from the other groups of people and I wonder if she knew any of them?

The door opens and Cynthia steps into the room with a very tall thin man. He is wearing a brown tweed jacket and he pushes a folded stethoscope into one of the pockets.

'This is Doctor Thompson,' she says. We all nod at him and Cynthia offers him a coffee.

He shakes his head. 'No thanks,' he says. 'I've got more patients to see so I'll have to head off straightaway. I simply wanted to let you all know the police have found Jenny's diary in the top of her case. She writes about cramp in her arm and a tight feeling in her chest. This corresponds with my findings that she probably had an undiagnosed heart condition and has died of a heart attack.'

Jane gasps loudly. 'Oh, the poor thing being all on her own when we were just along the corridor and could have helped!'

The elderly doctor shakes his head, but his blue eyes soften when he looks at Jane. 'No, I'm convinced this has been a sizeable heart attack and if it is any consolation, she probably wouldn't have known a great deal about it. She may well have died in seconds or even in her sleep without waking at all. Of course, we'll know more after the post-mortem which will need to take place because she has died away from her home.'

Cynthia smiles and touches the doctor's arm. She whimpers, 'Thank you so much for that, Doctor. It's a great relief for us to know Jenny hasn't suffered.'

Doctor Thompson nods. 'Well, the police have just about finished in the room and I've rang the undertakers so if anybody does want to see Jenny now is the time,' he says.

Jane and Stephen shake their heads abruptly as though the very thought is abhorrent to them. Bob stares down at his boots and shakes his head too.

I think of Jenny having no one with her when she died which was bad enough, but to be taken away to the mortuary alone just doesn't seem right. I blurt out, 'Yes! I'd like to see her please. I mean, I'd like to say my condolences.'

Biding us goodbye, Doctor Thompson strides from the room with Cynthia tottering along behind him.

Jane is sniffing into her tissue and Stephen steps up to the bar to order coffee for everyone.

I look at Bob who almost looks gleeful. His eyes are shining and the colour is back in his cheeks. 'Well, that's good to know,' he says patting the outside of his file. 'I thought it wouldn't be anything untoward and now we know for certain.'

He stretches out his legs and folds his arms across his puffed-out chest. 'I'll have a conversation with the police about how to make the arrangements. There may be a contact number on her mobile.'

I look sideways at Owen who shrugs his shoulders. I can tell he has noticed the change in Bob too. Stephen arrives with a coffee pot and the barman behind him carrying a tray with cups and saucers. We all sip the hot coffee and within half an hour Cynthia returns to escort me along the corridor back to room seven.

***

This time when we enter the room there is no dreadful shock. The curtains have been pulled back and the TV is switched off. Cynthia hovers at the doorway talking to the hotel manager as I approach the bed. Jenny is lying flat now without the pillows and a sheet over her body. The sheet is tucked under her chin and her eyes are closed.

'Poor Jenny,' I whisper close to her face. 'I'm so sorry that you've left us this way. I never did get to know you any better this weekend which I would have liked.'

My cheeks flush knowing this was because I'd been more engaged with Owen during the two days. I pull aside the sheet and smile at the flowery nightdress which reminds me of my grandma. I take her cold left hand in mine and squeeze it firmly. I know she won't be able to feel my hand, but it makes me feel better knowing she's had some type of human contact at her final demise.

I glance down at the other side of her thigh where her right hand is lying. A sudden ray of sunshine streams through the window. The sun glistens onto a shiny naval-brass button. I gasp knowing this is the missing button from Bob's jacket.

Printed in Great Britain
by Amazon

42680637R00030